This Yael book belongs to:

...........la5ky....♥..............

Yael Gets a Guest

Malky Weinstock

Illustrated by Steve Pileggi

This book is dedicated in loving memory to our unforgettable
Mother, Grandmother and Great-Grandmother

Mrs. Genendl bas Rav Shlomo **Berkowitz,** *zt"l*

Whose attributes, bravery, contentment, diligence, devotion, exertions, frugality,
gentleness, humaneness, love, intelligence, perseverance, quiet demeanor,
righteousness, simplicity, sincerity, tenacity, uniqueness, work ethic and wisdom
continue to inspire, motivate and energize our lives as we endeavor to walk in her
balanced path of דרך הממוצע.

Avrohom Pinchas and Mindy Berkowitz,
children and grandchildren, עמו"ש

Published by Lite Girl, Inc.
Text and illustrations © 2015 by Lite Girl, Inc.
www.bealitegirl.com

For updates, news, events, previews and special
introductory offers on new exciting LITE Girl
book releases and other products, sign up for FREE
membership now at www.bealitegirl.com

ISBN: 978-1-60763-190-3

Distributed by:
The Judaica Press, Inc.
www.judaicapress.com
800.972.6201

Summary: Yael's cousin Toby unexpectedly comes
to stay a while, and Yael struggles with sharing her
things, her space, and generally being gracious to
Toby. Through charming analogies and recalling the
hachnosas orchim (hospitality) exemplified by our
forefather Avraham, Yael gets it: "When you get a
guest, act your best!"

Credits:
Illustrations: Steve Pileggi/Blue Lion Designs
Cover design: Goldy Mermelstein
Editor: N. Shapiro
Audio CD produced and edited by Reuven A. Stone
Song recorded at Harlyn Studios (Celebration, FL)
Vocals recorded at UpTop Studio (Monsey, NY) and
engineered by Hillel Kapnick

Manufactured in China

Yael and her neighbors were outside, playing happily.

"Let's go inside," her mother said.

"Why now?" asked Yael. Fresh air breezed. Golden sun shined. She wished she didn't have to go now!

"A guest is coming! Cousin Toby's mother had a baby and she's coming to stay with us," Mommy told Yael.

Suddenly, the doorbell rang. Cousin Toby was here!

Yael wanted to go back outside to play.
But Toby was shy. She didn't want to go.

"Why not play inside with Toby?" Mommy suggested.

First, they played with the dolls. "I like your doll better!" Toby said. "She has nicer hair! Can I have it?"

It's MY *new birthday doll!* thought Yael.

"Let's play dress up now!" said Yael.
She quickly stuffed the dolls back
into the closet, onto the highest shelf.

Yael took out the dress-up trunk from the closet.
Plop. Plop. Out spilled a bunch of fun stuff!

"Oooh, this is fun!" giggled Toby. She put on a
red floppy hat. She tried on a flowy silver scarf.
She stepped into funny old shoes. Then she
picked out a gorgeous, sparkly necklace.

"Oh, wow! I love this necklace!" said Toby, fitting it over her head.

That's MY *special dress-up necklace that Savta gave me!* Yael wanted to shout.

Just then Mommy called out, "Supper time now, Yael and Toby!"

Yael quickly put the necklace away, hiding it under the pile of dress-up stuff.

At bedtime, Yael turned off all the lights.
But Toby wanted the hall light on.

"I'm afraid of the dark!" she whimpered.

Yael couldn't fall asleep with the light on.

It's **MY** *room!* Yael thought as she tossed and turned. *It's not fair!*

"When did you say Toby is leaving?" Yael whispered to her mother in the morning.

"I'm not in the mood of having a guest!"

"Oh, Yael!" said Mommy softly. "You never had a chance to have a guest before!"

"Did you know that welcoming guests, sharing our things with them and making them happy, is a great big mitzvah that Hashem wants us to do?

"We are all guests in Hashem's world, you know, and He shares so many favorite things with us to make us happy!"

"Hashem created the beautiful sun to warm us and make the world light.

"He created gorgeous flowers and a sky so blue to make our world pretty!

"And don't forget all the fruits and vegetables — pretty, delicious and oh so good for us! — that Hashem grows and shares with us!"

"Wow!" Yael thought. Pineapple was her favorite!

"Remember Avraham Avinu, the very first Jew?

"How he loved having guests! Every day, he waited for them and welcomed them. He put four open doors on his desert tent so guests could come in from every side!"

"He shared the place in his tent and all his favorite things. He even shared with his guests the yummiest food!

"Here's a rhyme to help you remember to welcome guests nicely every time — 'When you get a guest, act your best!'"

Toby came into the kitchen, her face sad and tearful.
She missed her mother and her new baby brother.

"I'm making a special breakfast because Toby's here!" announced
Mommy. "Heart-shaped toast with strawberry jam!"

"And pineapple for dessert!" chimed in Yael.

Toby's eyes lit up.

"Here, choose a school snack from this shelf,"
said Mommy after breakfast.

Toby reached in. She pulled out a big swirly lollipop.

That's MY lollipop that Great Aunt Bracha brought me!
Yael couldn't help but think, almost in tears.

But wait! "When you get a guest, act your best!" she suddenly remembered. Now she knew what she must do!

"It's the best lollipop you ever tasted!" Yael told Toby with a big smile.

"You let me have it?!" Toby couldn't believe it!

"Yes!" Yael said.

Toby hugged Yael.

"There's still time before the bus comes," said Yael.
"Let's draw a card for your mother and baby brother!"

Toby drew two girls holding hands. "That's me and you waving to my mother! I was afraid to come to be a guest. I can't wait to tell her how nice you were to me!"

Won't you act your best
when you get a guest?

Here are the Yael Gets a Guest song lyrics. Hope you'll sing along!
And remember, you can be a LITE GIRL, too!

(You can listen to the song being played on the Yael Gets a Guest CD.)

The doorbell is ringing — ring, ring, ring
Your guests have arrived! — sing, sing, sing
Roll out the red carpet.
The moment's finally here!
Welcome your guests with cheer, cheer, cheer.

(Talking piece:) Now tell me, what do LITE girls do
To make our guests feel happy, too?

CHORUS:
Like Avraham Avinu,
We love our guests.
Like Avraham Avinu,
We always treat them best.
And don't forget this secret —
LITE Girls know it's true —
When you take care of Hashem's children,
Hashem takes care of you!

Sharing your toys, your games, and your snacks.
Always make them want to come back.
They'll be happy for their visit.
So will you, 'cause you did-it, did-it, did-it!

(Talking piece:) Now tell me, what do LITE girls do
To make our guests feel happy, too?

CHORUS (2x):
Like Avraham Avinu,
We love our guests.
Like Avraham Avinu,
We always treat them best.
And don't forget this secret —
LITE Girls know it's true —
When you take care of Hashem's children,
Hashem takes care of you!

Also in the LITE Girl Series ...

A **lite girl** BOOK

Yael's Loving World

by Malky Weinstock
Illustrated by Steve Pileggi

love·inspire·teach·encourage

A **lite girl** BOOK

New Shoes for Yael

Audio/ Musical
CD Included!

by Malky Weinstock
Illustrated by Steve Pileggi

love·inspire·teach·encourage

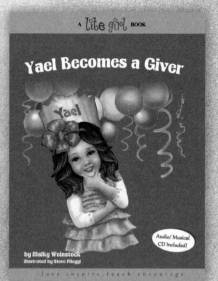

A **lite girl** BOOK

Yael Becomes a Giver

Audio/ Musical
CD Included!

by Malky Weinstock
illustrated by Steve Pileggi

love·inspire·teach·encourage

A **lite girl** BOOK

Yael Worries No More

Audio/ Musical
CD Included!

by Malky Weinstock
Illustrated by Steve Pileggi

love·inspire·teach·encourage

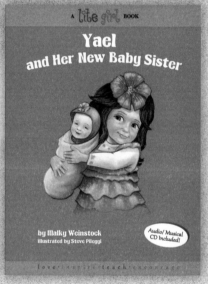

A **lite girl** BOOK

**Yael
and Her New Baby Sister**

by Malky Weinstock
illustrated by Steve Pileggi

Audio/ Musical
CD Included!

love·inspire·teach·encourage